# BORN IN A STABLE

**Tim Dowley**

**Illustrations by Gordon King**

## Mary's visitor
Many years ago there lived a young girl named Mary.
She lived with her family in a little town called Nazareth.
Mary was looking forward to her wedding.
She was going to marry Joseph the carpenter.
One day while Mary was busy in her house she heard a voice.
"Greetings!"
She looked up and to her surprise saw a stranger standing in the doorway.

## Good news
Mary was frightened.
She didn't know who it was talking to her.
"I.. er.."
"Don't be frightened, Mary," said the stranger.
"I have come with a message from God."
Mary felt even more frightened.
She knew the stranger must be an angel.
What could his message be?
"Mary, you mustn't be frightened," he repeated.
"I have good news for you.
God is going to give you a baby."
"But, but — I'm not even married yet," said Mary.
"How can this happen?"
"Mary, this is a very special baby.
God will make Him start to grow inside you."

## The baby's name

A baby son! A gift from God!
Mary could hardly believe her ears.
"Listen, Mary," said the angel.
"There is something else.
When your baby son is born,
you must call Him 'Jesus'."

"'*Jesus*'," Mary thought.
"Yes," she said, "that means 'God saves', doesn't it?"
Then the angel disappeared.
But Mary couldn't stop thinking about the angel's message.

## Mary visits her cousin

Mary was very excited.
But she was a bit worried too.
She wanted to talk to a friend who would understand how she felt.
Then she thought of just the right person — her cousin Elizabeth.
Elizabeth was a lot older than Mary.
In fact, she was past the age when women usually have babies.
But Mary had heard that Elizabeth too was expecting her first baby.
So Mary set out for the village in the hills where Elizabeth lived.

## Another baby

Elizabeth was very pleased to see Mary.
Even the baby inside Elizabeth jumped for joy when Mary arrived!
Elizabeth knew that Mary's baby was very special.
"Mary," she said. "How wonderful that the mother of my Lord should come to visit me!"
"I'm glad that you know my secret," said Mary.
Mary was so happy that she sang a song to thank God for promising her a baby.
"How good God is to His people," she sang.
Mary stayed until Elizabeth's baby boy was born.
Elizabeth called her baby John.

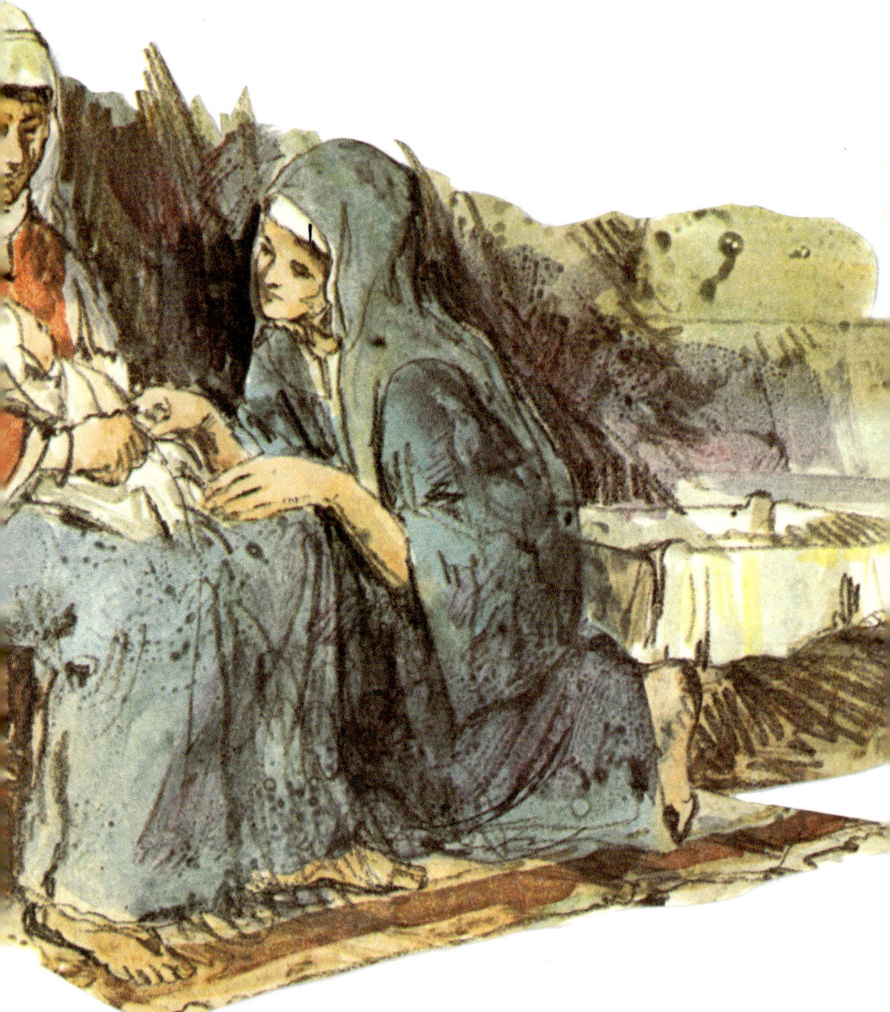

## Joseph's dream

When Joseph heard that Mary was going to have a baby he was very surprised.
Soon some of the people who lived nearby were saying unkind things about Mary.
So Joseph decided it would be best not to marry her after all.
But one night, while he was asleep, he had a special dream.
In his dream an angel said to him:
"Joseph, you must still marry Mary; her baby is from God.
You must call the baby Jesus.
He will save His people from their sins."
So Joseph did just as the angel told him, and he married Mary.

## A long journey

It was almost time for Mary's baby to be born.
But Joseph and Mary had to go back to Joseph's home-town Bethlehem to get their names on the king's list.
So Mary and Joseph set out on the long journey to Bethlehem.
Mary probably rode as best she could on a little donkey, and Joseph walked beside her.
They slept where they could on the journey, wrapped up in their warm coats.

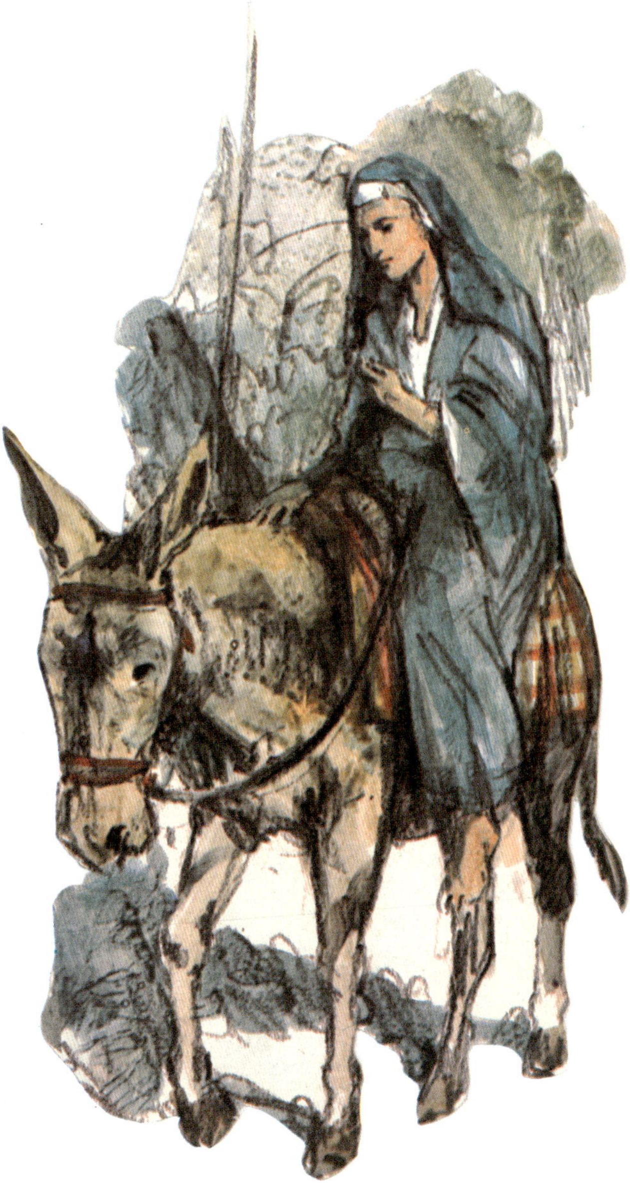

## Nowhere to sleep
Finally, after four or five days, Mary and Joseph arrived in Bethlehem.
They were both very tired, and Joseph asked where they could stay.
"There's no room," came the answer.
"There are lots of people here just now."
Joseph probably knocked on the door of the little hotel.
When a man came to the door, Joseph said:
"My wife is expecting a baby very soon.
Have you a room?"
The hotel-keeper shook his head.
"I'm sorry. We're completely full.
No empty rooms at all!"

## The baby is born
The man turned to go, but then perhaps he caught sight of Mary's tired face.
"Come with me," he may have said, leading them to the back of the hotel.
There they found a little stable where travellers' donkeys were resting.
"It's not very comfortable, but at least it's dry," said the man.
"You're welcome to it."
"Thank you," said Joseph and set about making Mary as comfortable as he could.
And there in the stable Mary's baby was born.
Mary wrapped her tiny baby in strips of cloth and put Him to sleep in the straw of the manger.

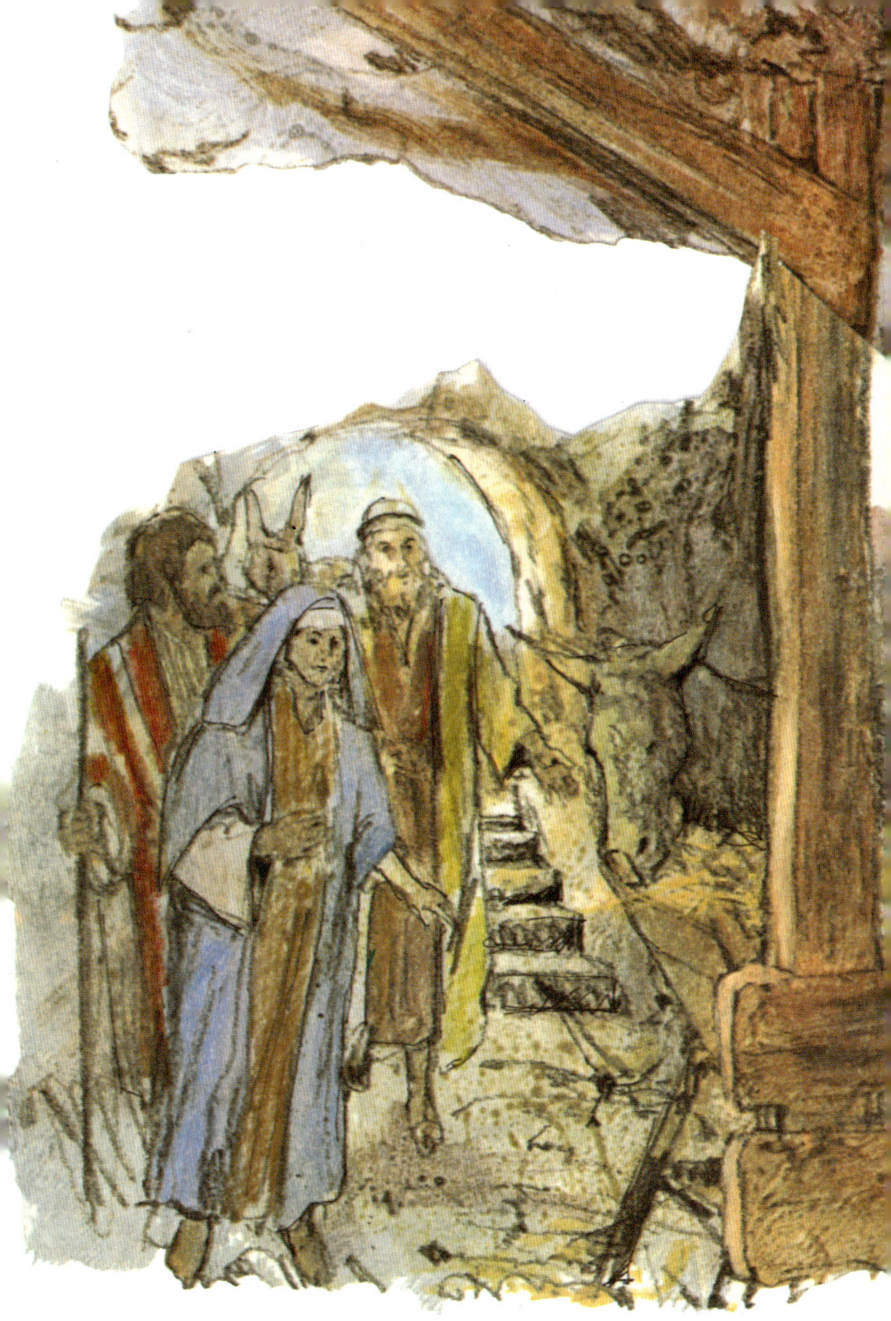

## The shepherds' visit

They may have been just settling down to sleep when there came a knock at the door.
Joseph went to see who was there.
"Is this where the baby is?" asked a man.
"Why — yes," said Joseph in surprise.
How did the man know that baby Jesus had been born in the stable?
"Can we come and see?"
Joseph let the man and his friends into the stable.
They crowded round to look at the baby asleep in the straw.

Then they explained why they had come.
"We are shepherds.
We were guarding our sheep on the hillside, when suddenly God's angel appeared.
He said 'Don't be afraid! This very day your Savior is born in Bethlehem! You will find the baby lying in a manger.'
And here He is!"

## An old man's thank-you

After this, the shepherds went back to look after their sheep on the hillside.

When Baby Jesus was just eight days old, Mary and Joseph took him to the Temple to give thanks to God.

Standing in the Temple was a very old man named Simeon.

He often came to the Temple.

He was waiting for God to send the Savior He had promised.

When Simeon saw Joseph and Mary with Baby Jesus, he knew this baby would grow up to become the Savior.

He took the baby in his arms and gave thanks to God. "Now I can die in peace," he said, "because I have seen with my own eyes the Savior promised by God."

## Visitors from far away

At the time Jesus was born, some wise men in a far country were studying the stars.
One of them noticed something strange.
"Look," he said. "A special star has come up in the east.
That means a new king is to be born."
So the wise men set out on a long journey across the desert to the land where Jesus was born.
They travelled on camels and carried expensive presents to give the new king.

When they reached the great city of Jerusalem,
they went to King Herod and asked:
"Where is the baby who is born to be the king of the Jews?"
But Herod was very angry; he was king of the Jews.
He didn't want any other kings in his land!
But Herod sent the wise men to Bethlehem.
There, at last, they found Baby Jesus.
The wise men knelt in front of the baby.
Then they gave Him their gifts; gold and rich
perfumes called frankincense and myrrh.

## Home to Nazareth

King Herod sent soldiers to try to find the Baby Jesus.

So Joseph and Mary ran away from Herod's land.

For long years Joseph, Mary, and Jesus lived in the land of Egypt.

Then Joseph had another special dream.

This time the angel told him it was safe to return home to Nazareth.

So Mary and Joseph and Jesus set out for home.

After another long journey, they finally arrived back in Nazareth.

## The carpenter's helper

They found a house to live in.

Before long the house was warm and clean.

Joseph soon set to work again as a carpenter, making furniture and tools for the people of Nazareth.

Little Jesus watched him.

And sometimes He helped Joseph with his work.

So Jesus was born safely in Bethlehem and grew up in Nazareth, because Mary and Joseph obeyed God.

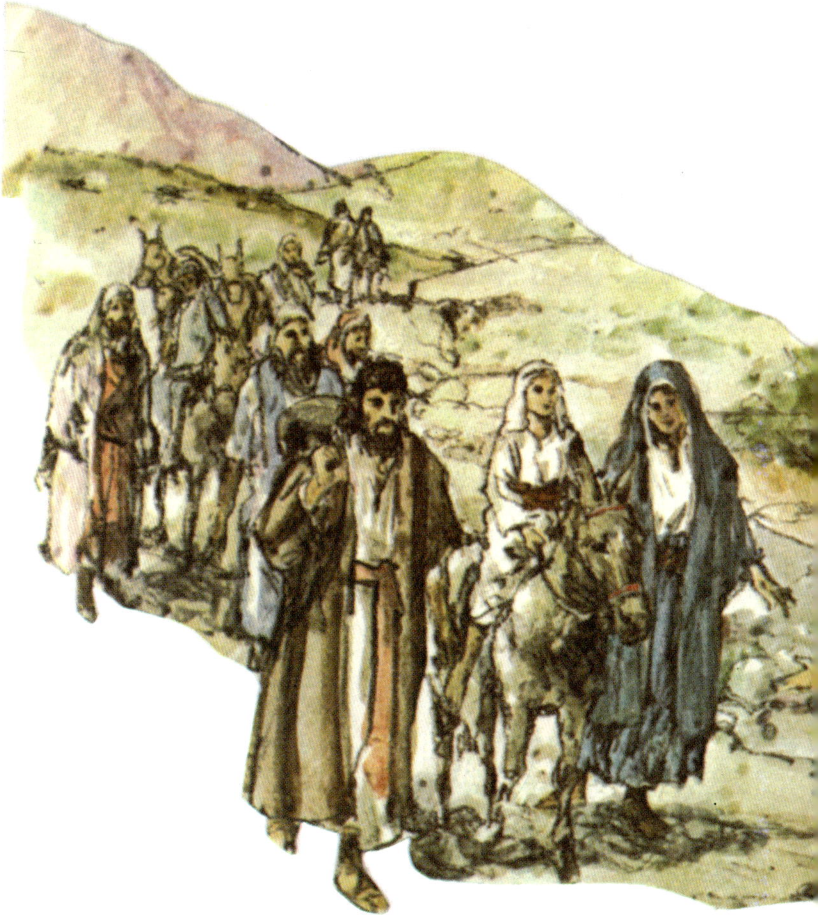

# For parents and teachers

**You can find these stories in your Bible.**

Mary's visitor: Luke 1:26-38
Mary visits her cousin: Luke 1:39-66
Joseph's dream: Matthew 1:18-25
A long journey: Luke 2:1-5
Nowhere to sleep: Luke 2:6-7
The shepherds' visit: Luke 2:8-20
An old man's thank-you: Luke 2:21-35
Visitors from far away: Matthew 2:1-12
Home to Nazareth: Matthew 2:13-23